This book is not intended as a substitute for the medical advice of trained and licensed physicians. Unless it's a really, really bad physician.

The Modern Joke Book

Copyright 2020 Mad Comedy

Spanish Homework

Kara's Spanish teacher was grading homework when she called Kara up to her desk.

"Kara, did you cheat on this Spanish homework? Did you use Google translate or some other app?"

"Oh, no, ma'am – I did it myself, just like you said."

"Really? Then why is your Spanish homework in French?"

Higher Ed

Q: How do you get someone with a Ph.D. in gender studies from Yale off your front porch?

A: Pay zir for the pizza.

The Caterpillars

Two caterpillars, high up a tree, are pursued by a hungry spider. They climb up a branch and get to the very end, but realize they are now trapped. They have nowhere to go, and the spider is approaching fast.

"Hold on tight!" says the first caterpillar, and he quickly chews through the branch.

The branch snaps and they begin to fall, but the caterpillar grabs two protruding leaves from the branch and uses them as wings to steer the branch through the air with grace and finesse.

"That's amazing!" says the second caterpillar. "How are you doing that?!"

The first caterpillar scoffs, "Am I the only one who still knows how to drive a stick?"

Shopping Green

A man called his husband and asked him to pick up some vegetables for that night's dinner on his way home from work.

"Make sure they're organic," he insisted. "We have to do the right thing for the planet."

The husband stopped at a grocery store and began to search all over for organic vegetables, but they didn't seem to be clearly marked.

Finally, he found a young man restocking broccoli in the produce department.

"Excuse me, I'm buying some vegetables for my husband. Have these been sprayed with poisonous chemicals?"

The produce guy looked up and said, "No sir, you'll have to do that yourself."

The Paint Job

A newly arrived immigrant, wanting to earn some money but lacking legal status to get a job, decided to hire herself out as a handyman-type and started canvassing a wealthy neighborhood. She went to the front door of the first house and asked the owner if he had any jobs for her to do.

"Well, I supposed you can paint my porch," the man said, sympathetic to the poor immigrant. "How much will you charge?"

The immigrant said, "How about 50 dollars?"

"For the whole porch?" the man said, astonished.

He readily agreed, and told her that the paint, brushes, and other materials that she might need were in the garage.

The man's wife, inside the house, heard the conversation and said to her husband, "Does she realize that the porch goes all the way around the house?"

The man replied, "She should, she was standing on it."

A short time later, the immigrant came to the door to collect her money.

"You're finished already?" he asked.

"Yes," the immigrant answered, "and I had paint left over, so I gave it two coats."

Impressed with her work ethic and efficiency, the man reached in his pocket for the $50, and he added another $20 as a tip.

The immigrant pocketed the money, and as she turned to leave, she said, "By the way, it's not a Porch. It's a Ferrari."

The Cure

A grown man in footy pajamas walked into a pharmacy and asked the pharmacist to give him something to cure the hiccups. The pharmacist eyed him and then leaned over the counter and slapped the guy, hard, right on his cheek.

"Why did you do that to me?" he complained.

"Well, you don't have the hiccups now, do you?"

"No, but my mom out in the car still does!" the man replied.

The Farmer

A bearded, tattooed millennial was out in the country practicing flying his drone. A farmer plowing a nearby field watched with bewilderment as a grown man played with a toy.

After a while, the millennial's watch alerted him that his train home was coming. He realized he'd never make it back to the station in time for his train unless he took a shortcut across the nearby farmer's field.

He asked the old farmer, "Hey, Boomer, would you mind if I crossed your field instead of going around it? I have to catch the 4:23 train."

The farmer shrugged and said, "Sure."

The millennial climbed the fence and started across the field toward the train station, carrying his expensive toy.

When he got nearly halfway across the field, the farmer called after him, "And if my bull sees you, you'll even catch the 4:11 train!"

Chinese Freedom

Everyone says that China doesn't have any freedom of speech. That's obviously untrue.

In the United States, you can go up to the White House and shout, "Death to America!", and you won't be punished for it.

Similarly, in China, you can go up to the Communist Party Headquarters and shout, "Death to America!" and you won't be punished for it.

Baruti and his Elephant

Baruti was a boy who live in a small village in Botswana in Africa. Botswana is famous for its native wildlife, especially African Elephants. Baruti would spend days watching the wild animals on the plain, learning and studying their behaviors.

Twice a year, when the great animal migration passed through, the villagers would gather their meagre belongings and hide in caves in the hills above their village. When they returned, they would find that their village had been ravaged by marauding elephants that would trample their crops and even tear apart their simple mud-and-straw huts.

After one especially devastating year when the village was almost completely destroyed, Baruti vowed to learn as much as he could about elephants to help his village.

One day as he sat hidden in the tall grass, he saw an enormous mature bull elephant with a broken tusk that appeared to be in distress. As Baruti crawled as close as he could to observe the elephant, he noticed that the elephant was holding one foot off the ground. Baruti crawled closer still and saw there was blood on the elephant's foot.

Scared but determined, Baruti stood and approached the elephant and saw a large thorn stuck in the elephant's foot. Screwing up his courage, Baruti held the elephant's huge foot in one hand and with the other hand pulled at the thorn with all his might. The thorn came loose at last. Baruti gave a shout of triumph and the elephant gave a loud trumpet.

Suddenly the elephant wrapped his trunk around Baruti and lifted him high off the ground. Baruti and the elephant looked at each other. Baruti saw joy and thankfulness in the elephant's wise old eyes. After a few touching moments, the elephant gently placed Baruti on the ground and stamped his front foot on the ground three times and slowly turned and walked away.

After that day, Baruti vowed to double his efforts to

learn all he could about the elephants. Soon he became famous for his knowledge throughout the land and was invited by neighboring villages and cities and countries to talk about his experiences.

Many years later, Baruti was now an old man. He'd become the world's foremost expert on elephants. But he was more than that. He'd become a celebrated global star, championing causes ranging from animal rights to climate change to fighting racism.

But after his long and storied career, Baruti was tired. He decided it was time to go home. He found himself back in the village he had lived in as a child. But it was no longer just a simple small village of mud huts. It was a modern city filled with all the trappings of modernity and a million people. It even had its own zoo.

Baruti decided to visit the zoo. Baruti walked around the animal enclosures smiling, remembering his life as a boy, when suddenly behind him he heard an elephant blow his trumpet.

Baruti turned and saw an ancient elephant with a broken task with its trunk raised. They looked at each other, and then the elephant stamped its feet on the ground three times. Baruti could not believe it! His heart was filled with joy. His life had come full circle.

Old Baruti hobbled closer to the old elephant, and they looked at each other. Baruti raised his hands over the fence and hugged the elephant's thick trunk. The elephant wrapped his trunk around Baruti and lifted him off the ground and over the fence, and once again Baruti could stare into those wise old elephant eyes.

Suddenly the elephant threw Baruti hard onto the ground and stomped on Baruti's head three times, killing him.

It was a different elephant.

Russian Problems

Vladimir Putin is visiting a big factory in Kazan, Russia, for a photo op with the international media, and he decides to use the common man to demonstrate all the progress Russia has made under his leadership.

He walks up to one of the line workers and says, "My friend, I hear alcoholism used to be a big problem in Russia. Tell me, do you think you could still do your job if you drank a bottle of vodka in the morning?"

The worker shrugs and says, "Yes, I suppose so."

Putin frowns because that wasn't the answer he was expecting, but he knew the international media was watching, so he presses on: "Do you think you could still do your job if you'd had two bottles of vodka in the morning?"

The worker nods and says he probably could.

Putin, now becoming exasperated, asks: "What if you'd had three bottles?"

The worker replies, "I'm here, aren't I?"

The Birth of Jesus

On the night of the birth of Jesus, the baby was asleep in the manger and Mary and Joseph were resting when three wise men arrived bearing gifts.

As the second wise man stepped into the barn, he hit his head on the low ceiling.

"Jesus Christ!" the wise man shouted, rubbing his head.

"Write that down," Mary said to Joseph. "It sounds much better than Kevin."

Bad News

A policeman knocked on the door, and a woman answered.

"Yes, officer?"

The policeman took off his hat and said softly, "I'm very sorry, ma'am, but it looks like your wife got hit by a bus."

"I'm aware of that," the woman replied, "but Becky has a wonderful personality."

The Gardener

Once there was a beautiful woman who loved working in her organic vegetable garden, but no matter what she did, she couldn't get her organic tomatoes to ripen. Admiring her neighbor's garden, which had beautiful bright red organic tomatoes, she stopped over one day and asked him his secret.

"It's really quite simple," the old man explained. "Twice each day, in the morning and in the evening, I expose myself in front of the tomatoes and they turn red with embarrassment."

Desperate for the perfect organic garden, she tried his advice and proceeded to expose herself to her plants twice daily. Two weeks later, her neighbor stopped by to check her progress.

"So," he asked, "any luck with your tomatoes?"

"No," she replied excitedly, "but you should see the size of my cucumbers!"

The Vegan

A young college man was a vegan, having sworn off all manner of animal products, and loudly proclaimed to anyone within earshot on campus that eating meat was tantamount to murder. He became quite vocal on social media, leading a campaign to restrict meat and meat products. He was elected to the student council based on his passionate vegan beliefs.

But despite all that, he couldn't help thinking about just a little bit of pork. Delicious, crispy bacon. A ham sandwich. A pork chop.

Over time, the desire overwhelmed him. He had to have some pork. Of course, if anyone saw him, he'd be ruined, so he had to do it in secret.

He decided to take an Uber way out of town to a restaurant where no one would see him. After sitting down and perusing the menu, he ordered a roasted pig, and impatiently waited for his delicacy.

After just a few minutes, he heard someone call his name. To his great chagrin, he saw that several of the leading campus vegetarians and vegans were walking towards him!

Just at that same moment, the waiter walked over carrying a huge platter holding a full roasted pig with an apple in its mouth.

The young man paused, looking up at his friends. The smell of roasted pork hung in the air. The juicy red apple glimmered in the pig's mouth.

"Can you believe this?" he says. "All I ordered was an apple!"

Kickstarter

A heartfelt plea on Kickstarter to help a family in need received tremendous support. Hundreds of contributors reacted to the description of the family:

"There is a family that I know very well that is in desperate need of money. The poor father has been out of a job for over a year, they have five kids at home with barely a bit of food to eat. The worst part is, that they are about to kicked out of their house and they will be left on the streets without a roof over their heads! They need $3,000 to pay their back rent."

In a matter of days, the $3,000 was collected from generous souls.

One person commented on Kickstarter, "That's such a sad story. How do you know the family?"

"I'm their landlord," was the reply.

The Legal Mind

A rich and influential lawyer finds out he has a brain tumor, and it's inoperable. In fact, it's so large, he needs a brain transplant.

His doctor gives him a choice of available brains: there's a jar of engineers' brains for $100 an ounce, a jar of programmers' brains for $150 an ounce, and a jar of lawyers' brains for the princely sum of $8,000 an ounce.

The lawyer smiled, "I knew it! Lawyers are the best and brightest! That's why our brains are so valuable, right?"

The doctor replies, "Not exactly. Do you know how many lawyers it takes to get an ounce of brains?"

The Park Ranger

A park ranger in Alaska is giving some hikers a warning about bears, "Black bears are usually harmless. They avoid contact with humans, so we suggest you attach small bells to your backpacks and give the bears time to get out of your way."

The group of hikers all nodded.

The park ranger continued, "However, grizzly bears are extremely dangerous. If you see any grizzly bear droppings, leave the area immediately."

"So how do we know if they're grizzly bear droppings?" asks one of the hikers.

"It's easy," replies the ranger. "They're full of small bells."

Talking Dog

A guy read a Facebook ad for a talking dog for sale. Intrigued, he contacts the owner and goes over to see if it could really be true. The owner opens the door and introduces him to his dog.

"Hello," the dog says.

The man is shocked.

"You can actually talk?" the incredulous man asks, looking around for some kind of trick.

"Sure," says the dog, "in fact, I'm fluent in seven languages."

"Seven languages! Astounding!"

"Yes," says the dog, licking his paw, "and I'm finishing up my Ph.D. dissertation at Harvard. Of course, it's tough to get it done with all the time I'm spending working with our Special Forces hunting terrorists, and of course my hobby rescuing lost skiers and hikers in avalanches."

"Wow," the man says, flabbergasted.

He asks the dog's owner, "Why on earth would you want to get rid of an incredible dog like that?"

The owner says, "Because he's a liar! He never did any of that stuff!"

Divorce Pending

A man in California texts his son in New York the day before Christmas Eve and types, "Son, I hate to ruin your day, but I have to tell you that your mother and I are divorcing; forty-five years of misery is enough."

"Dad, what are you talking about?" the son texts angrily back.

"We can't stand the sight of each other any longer," the father texts. "We're sick of each other and I'm sick of talking about this, so you call your sister in Miami and tell her."

Frantically, the son calls his sister, who explodes on the phone.

"Like hell they're getting divorced!" she shouts. "I'll take care of this!"

She calls California immediately, and screams at her father, "You are NOT getting divorced! Don't do a single thing until I get there. I'm calling my brother back, and we'll both be there tomorrow. Until then, don't do a thing, DO YOU HEAR ME?!?"

The old man hangs up his phone and turns to his wife.

"Good news! They're both coming home for Christmas -- and they're paying their own way."

Dying of Thirst

After his plane crash-landed, a man was lost in the desert. His phone had no signal, so he had no choice but to find his way out.

For days he wandered across the burning sands looking for a town, a village, or an oasis. He was tortured by thirst when finally, in the distance, he saw a man riding a camel. He struggled to climb and descend several dunes and finally approached the man.

"Water," he said. "Please... water."

"I have no water," said the man on the camel. "But I will sell you a necktie for $10."

The thirsty man looked at him like he was crazy. "A necktie? You insensitive jerk! Can't you see I'm dying of thirst? Get the hell out of here!"

The man on the camel rode away.

The thirsty man crawled over a few more dunes, his mouth dry, his lips chapped. He couldn't go much further.

Finally, from the top of one of the largest dunes in the desert, he saw a beautiful country club in the middle of a green oasis just below him! It had a large world-class golf course, with sprinklers keeping the grass a brilliant green, an Olympic-size swimming pool with people splashing and diving in it, an outdoor bar with the bartender handing out ice-cold beers, waiters circulating among the sunbathers with trays of cold drinks, and a large fountain spewing crystal-clear water ten feet into the air.

Desperate, the man crawled down to the gate.

"Water," he said, his voice cracking, to the man at the gate. "I need... water."

"Sorry, sir, but I can't let you in without a necktie," said the guard.

Horse Auction

Little Johnny attended a horse auction with his father. He watched as his father moved from horse to horse, running his hands up and down the horse's legs and rump and chest.

After a few minutes, Johnny asked, "Dad, why are you doing that?"

His father replied, "When I'm buying horses, I have to make sure that they are healthy and in good shape before I spend money on them."

Johnny, looking worried, said, "Dad, I think the Amazon delivery guy wants to buy Mom."

Sherlock Holmes

Sherlock Holmes and Dr. Watson go on a camping trip. After a nice dinner prepared over the campfire, they retire for the night, and go to sleep. Some hours later, Holmes wakes up and nudges his faithful friend.

"Watson, look up at the sky and tell me what you see."

"I see millions and millions of stars, Holmes," exclaims Watson.

"And what do you deduce from that?"

Watson ponders for a minute.

"Well, astronomically, it tells me that there are millions of galaxies and potentially billions of planets. Astrologically, I observe that Saturn is in Leo. Horologically, I deduce that the time is approximately a quarter past three. Meteorologically, I suspect that we will have a beautiful day tomorrow. Theologically, I can see that God is all powerful, and that we are a small and insignificant part of the universe. What does it tell you, Holmes?"

And Holmes said, "Watson, you idiot, it tells me that somebody stole our tent."

The Cherry Tree

A farmer grabbed his 10-year-old son and asked, "Did you cut down that cherry tree?"

"Yes, Daddy, I did," the boy replied. "I cannot tell a lie."

The farmer grabbed the boy, put him over his knee, and spanked the tar out of him.

"But, Daddy!" the boy cried, "George Washington's father didn't do that to him when he cut down that cherry tree when he was a boy."

"That's true," the father replied, "but George Washington's father wasn't sitting in the tree when he cut it down!"

Circus Freaks

A husband and wife who work for the circus went to an adoption agency looking to adopt a child, but the social workers there raised doubts about their suitability. The couple knew their traveling circus lifestyle would raise questions, so they were well-prepared.

The couple produced photos of their 50-foot motor home, which was clean and well maintained and equipped with a beautiful nursery.

The social workers were satisfied with this, but then raised concerns about the kind of education a child would receive while in the couple's care.

The husband put them at ease, saying, "We've arranged for a full-time tutor who will teach the child all the usual subjects along with French, Mandarin, and of course coding."

Next though, the social workers expressed concerns about the safety and well-being of a child raised in a circus environment.

This time the wife explains, "We have engaged a full-time nanny who is a certified expert in pediatric care, child welfare, and healthy dietary practices."

The social workers were finally satisfied and asked the couple, "What age and gender child are you hoping to adopt?"

The husband said, "Oh, it doesn't really matter, as long as the kid fits in the cannon."

The Waiter

The man takes his family out to a fancy restaurant for dinner. The man orders soup as an appetizer, but when the waiter brings the soup to the table, the waiter is holding the bowl with his thumb in the soup.

The man looks up, disgusted, and demands, "Why is your thumb in my soup?"

The waiter says, "Last night the chef dropped a pot on my hand, injuring my thumb, and the first aid app on my phone said to keep it in a warm place to ease the swelling."

The man was shocked, and said, "You idiot! Instead of my soup, stick your thumb where the sun don't shine!"

The waiter responds, "Well, I had it up there, but I needed both hands to serve your soup."

Amish Lesson

A fifteen-year-old Amish boy and his father were in a mall. They were amazed by everything they saw, but especially by two shiny silver walls that could move apart and then slide back together again.

The boy asked, "What is this thing, Father?"

The father, having never seen an elevator, shrugged, "Son, I have never seen anything like this in my life. I have no idea what it is."

While the boy and his father were watching with amazement, a fat old lady in a wheel chair moved up to the moving walls and pressed a button. The walls opened, and the lady rolled between them into a small room. The walls closed, and the boy and his father watched the small numbers above the walls light up sequentially. They continued to watch until it reached the last number, and then the numbers began to light in the reverse order.

Finally the walls opened up again and a gorgeous 24-year-old blonde in a miniskirt stepped out.

The father, not taking his eyes off the young woman, said quietly to his son, "Go get your Mother."

CIA Assassin

The CIA had an open position for an assassin. After all the background checks, interviews and testing were completed, they had narrowed the field down to three possible agents.

For the final test, the CIA agents took one of the three candidates to a large metal door and handed him a gun.

"We must know that you will follow your instructions no matter what the circumstances. Inside the room you will find your wife sitting in a chair. We need you to kill her."

The man said, "You can't be serious. I could never shoot my wife."

The agent said, "Then you're not the right man for this job. Take your wife and go home."

The second man was given a gun and told to go shoot his husband. He took the gun and went into the room. All was quiet for about five minutes.

The man came out with tears in his eyes, "I tried, but I can't kill my husband."

The agent said, "You don't have what it takes. Take your husband home."

Finally, the last candidate, a woman, was given the same instructions: to kill her wife. She took the gun and went into the room. Shots were heard, one after another. Then they heard screaming, crashing, and banging on the walls. After a few minutes, all was quiet.

The door opened slowly and there stood the woman, wiping the sweat from her brow.

"Some idiot loaded the gun with blanks," she said. "I had to strangle her to death."

Musk's Conference

Billionaire technology entrepreneur Elon Musk's bodyguard looks a little bit like him. One day, Musk had to speak at an important science conference.

Riding in the back of his self-driving car on the way there, Musk tells his bodyguard, "I'm so sick of all these conferences. I always say the same things over and over!"

The bodyguard agrees, "You're right. As your bodyguard, I've attended all of them with, and even though I don't know anything about technology, I feel like I could give the presentation in your place."

"That's a great idea!" laughs Musk. "Let's switch places then!"

As soon as they arrive, they switch clothes. The bodyguard, dressed as Elon Musk, goes on stage and starts giving the usual speech, while the real Musk, dressed as the bodyguard, sits in the audience, delighted.

But in the crowd sits one of Musk's rivals who wants to impress everyone – and humiliate Musk. He thinks of a very difficult question to ask Musk, hoping he won't be able to respond. With all the media watching, Musk will be humiliated.

So the guy stands up and interrupts the conference by posing his very difficult technical question. The whole room goes silent, holding their breath, waiting for the response.

The fake Musk looks down at the questioner from the stage, eyeing him for a moment before replying, "Sir, your question is elementary that I'm going to let my bodyguard answer it for me."

New Laws

By legalizing same-sex marriage and Marijuana, Colorado has finally interpreted the Bible verse from Leviticus 20:13 correctly: "If a man lies with another man, he should be stoned."

The Zipper

In a crowded city at a busy bus stop, a beautiful young woman wearing a tight leather skirt with a long zipper up the back was waiting for a bus. As the bus stopped and it was her turn to get on, she became aware that her skirt was too tight to allow her leg to come up to the height of the first step of the bus.

Slightly embarrassed and with a quick smile to the bus driver, she reached behind her to unzip her skirt a little, thinking that this would give her enough slack to raise her leg. She tried to again take the step, only to discover that she couldn't.

So, a little more embarrassed, she once again reached behind her to unzip her skirt a little more, and for the second time attempted the step. Once again, much to her embarrassment she could not raise her leg.

With a little smile to the driver, she again reached behind to unzip a little more and again was unable to take the step.

About this time, a large guy who was standing behind her picked her up easily by the waist and placed her gently on the step of the bus.

The young lady went ballistic and turned to the would-be Samaritan and screeched, "How dare you touch my body! I'm a proud independent feminist and my body is mine. I do not consent to your white-privileged patriarchic touching!"

The guy smiled and said with a syrupy Southern drawl, "Well, ma'am, normally I would agree with you, but after you unzipped my fly three times, I kinda figured you'd given me affirmative consent."

The Diagnosis

After reviewing her test results, the doctor told his patient, "I'm sorry but you suffer from a terminal illness and have only ten to live."

The patient looks up in horror, "What do you mean, ten? Ten what? Ten years? Ten months?? Ten weeks?!?"

The Doctor responded, "Nine."

The Shrink

A man goes to a psychiatrist in a terrible state.

"Doc, Doc, I keep have these recurring dreams. In my dream, first I'm a yurt, then I'm a teepee. Over and over, I'm a yurt, then a teepee. Every night, it's the same thing. I can't get any sleep! What's the matter with me?"

The psychiatrist looks down over his glasses at his patient and says, "It's simple. You're two tents."

Service Rivalry

Two Marines boarded a flight out of Atlanta headed to San Antonio. One sat in the window seat, the other sat in the middle seat. Just before take-off, an Army soldier got on and took the aisle seat next to the two Marines.

As the plane took off and reached cruising altitude, the Army soldier kicked off his shoes, wiggled his toes and was settling in when the Marine in the window seat said, "I think I'll get up and get a Coke."

"No problem," said the Army soldier in the aisle seat, "I'll get it for you."

While he was gone, the Marine picked up the soldier's shoe and spit in it.

When the soldier returned with the Coke, the Marine in the middle seat said, "That looks good, I think I'll have one too."

Again, the soldier obligingly went to fetch the drink, and while he was gone, the second Marine picked up the soldier's other shoe and spit in it.

The soldier returned and they all sat back and enjoyed the rest of the flight to San Antonio. As the plane was landing, the soldier slipped his feet into his shoes and knew immediately what had happened.

"How long must this go on?" the Soldier mused. "This fighting between our services? This hatred? This animosity? This spitting in shoes -- and peeing in Cokes?"

Pulled Over

A policeman on a motorcycle pulls over a car.

"What's the matter, officer?" asks the driver.

"Your wife fell out of your passenger door three miles back!" says the policeman.

"Thank goodness for that," says the driver. "I thought I'd gone deaf."

Lesson Learned

Finding one of her students making faces at others on the playground, Ms. Smith stopped to gently reprimand the child.

Smiling sweetly, the Sunday school teacher said, "Johnny, when I was a little girl, I was told if that I made ugly faces, it would freeze and I would stay like that."

Little Johnny looked up and replied, "Well, Ms. Smith, you can't say you weren't warned."

The Burglar

A man went to the police station wishing to speak with the burglar who had broken into his house the night before.

"Sorry, sir, you'll get your chance to confront him in court," said the Desk Sergeant.

"No, no, no," said the man. "I want to know how he got into the house without waking my wife. I've been trying to do that for years!"

Old Married Couple

A couple drove down a country road for several miles, not saying a word. An earlier discussion had led to an argument and neither of them wanted to concede their position.

As they passed a barnyard of mules, goats, and pigs, the husband asked sarcastically, "Relatives of yours?"

"Yep," the wife replied, "My in-laws."

The Loan

Before going to Europe on business, a man drove his Rolls Royce to a downtown New York City bank and went in to ask for an immediate loan of $5,000. The loan officer was surprised, and requested collateral.

"Well, then, here are the keys to my Rolls-Royce," the man said.

The loan officer promptly had the car driven into the bank's underground parking garage for safekeeping, and gave the man his $5,000 loan. Two weeks later, the man walked through the bank's doors, and asked to settle up his loan and get his car back.

The loan officer checked the records and told him, "That will be $5,000 in principal, and, let's see, two weeks of interest comes to $19.82."

The man wrote out a check, thanked the loan officer, and started to walk away.

"Wait sir," the loan officer said, "while you were gone, I found out you are a rich businessman with millions deposited in this bank. Why in the world would you need to borrow $5,000?"

The man smiled, "Where else could I securely park my Rolls-Royce in Manhattan for two weeks and pay only $19.82?"

Soldier's Pitch

Private Jones was assigned to the induction center, where he advised new recruits about their government benefits, especially their GI life insurance. It wasn't long before Captain Smith noticed that Private Jones was having a staggeringly high success rate, selling GI life insurance to nearly 100% of the recruits he advised.

Rather than ask about this, the Captain stood in the back of the room and listened to Jones' sales pitch.

Jones explained the basics of the GI Insurance to the new recruits, and then said: "If you have GI life insurance and go into battle and are killed, the government has to pay $200,000 to your beneficiaries. If you don't have GI insurance, and you go into battle and get killed, the government only has to pay a maximum of $6,000."

"Now," Airman Jones concluded, "which group do you think they are going to send into battle first?"

New Drill Instructor

One of my husband's duties as a novice drill instructor at Fort Jackson, S.C., was to escort new recruits to the mess hall.

After everyone had made it through the chow line, he sat them down and told them, "There are three rules in this mess hall: Shut up! Eat up! Get up!"

Checking to see that he had everyone's attention, he demanded, "What is the first rule?"

Much to the amusement of the other instructors, sixty privates yelled in unison, "Shut up, Drill Sergeant!"

Church Troubles

An elderly couple was attending church services.

About halfway through the sermon, the little old lady leaned over to her husband and whispered, "I just passed a little gas. Don't worry, it was silent, no one heard me."

He turned to her and replied, "We need to change the battery in your hearing aid."

Merry Christmas

When four of Santa's elves got sick, the trainee elves did not produce toys as fast as the regular ones, and Santa began to feel the pre-Christmas pressure.

Then Mrs. Claus told Santa that her Mother was coming to visit, which stressed Santa even more.

When he went to harness the reindeer, he found that three of them were about to give birth and two others had jumped the fence and were missing.

Then when he began to load the sleigh, one of the floorboards cracked, the toy bag fell to the ground and all the toys were scattered.

Frustrated, Santa went in the house for a cup of apple cider and a shot of rum. When he went to the cupboard, he discovered the elves had drunk all the cider and hidden the liquor.

In his frustration, he accidentally dropped the cider jug, and it broke into hundreds of little glass pieces all over the kitchen floor.

He went to get the broom and found the mice had eaten all the straw off the end of the broom.

Just then the doorbell rang, and an irritated Santa marched to the door, yanked it open, and there stood a little angel with a great big Christmas tree.

The angel said very cheerfully, "Merry Christmas, Santa. Isn't this a lovely day? I have a beautiful tree for you. Where would you like me to stick it?"

And thus began the tradition of the little angel stuck on top of the Christmas tree.

Impressive Golfer

A guy stands over his tee shot for what seems an eternity: looking up, looking down, measuring the distance, figuring the wind direction and speed.

Finally his exasperated partner says, "What's taking so long? Hit the darn ball!"

The guy answers, "My wife is up there watching me from the clubhouse. I want to make this a perfect shot."

"Forget it, man," says his partner. "You'll never hit her from here."

The Break-In

Late one night, a burglar broke into a house he thought was empty.

He tiptoed through the living room but suddenly he froze in his tracks when he heard a loud voice say, "Jesus is watching you!"

Silence returned to the house, so the burglar crept forward again.

"Jesus is watching you," the voice boomed again.

The burglar stopped dead again, frightened. Frantically, he looked all around. In a dark corner, he spotted a bird cage and in the cage was a parrot.

He asked the parrot, "Was that you who said Jesus is watching me?"

"Yes," said the parrot.

The burglar breathed a sigh of relief and asked the parrot, "What's your name?"

"Clarence," said the bird.

"That's a dumb name for a parrot," sneered the burglar. "What idiot named you Clarence?"

The parrot said, "The same idiot who named the Rottweiler 'Jesus'."

The Dentist's Chair

A man had been putting off going to the dentist for some time, but finally the pain in his tooth was unbearable. The dentist had him sit in the chair and open wide. He probed the aching tooth, which made the man wince.

"I'm afraid this is going to hurt," the dentist said.

The man in the chair mumbled, "Go ahead, I can take it."

"I'm sleeping with your wife," the dentist said.

Old Farts

A hunting lodge was having trouble attracting new members, and all the existing members were getting very, very old. So the lodge extended membership offers to Millennials whose only hunting experience was in video games.

One night in the elaborate hunting lodge lined with the mounted, stuffed kills from successful hunts, two new video game hunting members were being introduced to other members and shown around.

The man leading them around said, "See that old man asleep in the chair by the fireplace? He is our oldest member and can tell you some hunting stories you'll never forget."

They awakened the old man and asked him to tell them a hunting story.

"Well," he began, "I remember back in 1964, we went on a lion hunting expedition in Africa."

The old man paused, thinking, and continued, "We were on foot and hunted for three days without seeing a thing. On the fourth day, I was so tired I had to rest. I found a fallen tree, so I laid my gun down, propped my head on the tree, and fell asleep. I don't know how long I was asleep when I was awakened by a noise in the bushes. I was reaching for my gun when the biggest lion I ever seen jumped out of the bushes at me like this, 'ROOOAAAAARR!'"

The old man paused, looked up at the young men, and said, "I tell you, I just crapped my pants."

The young men looked astonished, and one of them said, "I don't blame you, I would have crapped my pants too if a lion jumped out at me."

The old man shook his head and said, "No, no, not back then in Africa. Right now when I said 'ROOOAAAAARR!'"

The Golfers

Andre and John were out golfing, and as they were playing the fifth hole, Andre turned to John and said, "Those two guys on the sixth tee are too slow. Why don't you run up there and ask if we can play through?"

John jogged up to the sixth tee, and just before he got there, he turned and ran back to Andre as fast as his legs could carry him!

"I can't talk to those guys! One of them is my husband and the other is my boyfriend! You go up and ask them!"

So Andre jogged up to the sixth tee, and just before he got there, he turned and ran back as fast as his legs could carry him!

As he approached John, he exclaimed, "By God, it's a small world, isn't it?"

Car Sale

A sixteen-year-old boy came home with a new Porsche and his parents, shocked, demanded, "Where did you get that car?!"

He calmly told them, "I bought it today."

"With what money?" asked his stunned parents.

They knew what a Porsche cost. There was no way a teenager could afford one.

"Well," said the boy, "this one cost me just fifteen dollars."

His parents began to yell even louder.

"Who would sell a car like that for fifteen dollars?" they demanded.

"It was the lady up the street," said the boy. "I don't know her name - they just moved in. She saw me ride past on my bike and asked me if I wanted to buy a Porsche for fifteen dollars."

"Oh my goodness!" moaned the mother, "she must be a child abuser. Who knows what she will do next? John, you go right up there and see what's going on."

So the boy's father walked up the street to the house where the lady lived and found her out in the yard calmly collecting the mail from the mailbox. He introduced himself as the father of the boy to whom she had sold a new Porsche for fifteen dollars and demanded to know why she did it.

"Well," she said, "this morning I got a phone call from my husband. I thought he was on a business trip, but learned from a friend he had run off to Hawaii with his mistress and doesn't intend to come back."

"I'm sorry to hear that," the man said. "But what does that have to do with the Porsche you sold to my son?"

"Well, my husband claimed he was stranded and needed cash, and asked me to sell his new Porsche and send him the money. So I did."

Help from God

A major storm blew in, leading to massive flooding right up to the rooftops. There was a preacher perched on top of his church, stranded, and the water was still rising.

When a boat came by, the captain yelled, "Do you need help, sir?"

The preacher calmly said, "No, God will save me."

A little later, another boat came by and a fisherman asked, "Hey, do you need help?"

The preacher replied again, "No, God will save me."

Eventually the preacher drowned and went to heaven.

The preacher asked God, "Why didn't you save me?"

God replied, "Hey, dummy, I sent you two boats!"

Speeding Ticket

A man in his mid-forties bought a new BMW and was out on the interstate for a nice evening drive. The top was down, the breeze was blowing through what was left of his hair and he decided to see what the engine had.

As the needle jumped up to 80 mph, he suddenly saw flashing red and blue lights behind him.

"There's no way they can catch a BMW," he thought to himself and opened her up further.

The needle hit 90, then 100, and finally reality hit him and he knew he shouldn't run from the police, so he slowed down and pulled over. The cop came up to him, took his license without a word and examined it and the car.

"It's been a long day, this is the end of my shift and it's Friday the 13th. I don't feel like more paperwork, so if you can give me an excuse for your driving that I haven't heard before, you can go."

The guy thinks for a second and says, "Last week my wife ran off with a cop. I was afraid you were trying to bring her back."

"Have a nice weekend," said the officer as he walked away.

The Lyft Driver

Having gotten too old to drive, every day at 11 am an old grandma uses the phone her grandson gave her to order a Lyft to pick her up and take her to her bridge game at the club. Every day, she gets the same driver. And every day, she slowly climbs into the back of the car and offers the driver a bag of peanuts.

The Lyft driver happily accepts, and munches on peanuts throughout the ride. This went on for weeks.

At first, the driver enjoyed the peanuts, but after a few weeks of eating them, he asked the old woman not to bring him any more peanuts.

"I appreciate it, but please don't bring me peanuts. Enjoy them yourself."

"Oh, no, I can't eat them!" she said.

"Why not?" the driver asked.

The granny answers: "Well, I don't have my teeth anymore, so I just suck the chocolate off and give the peanuts to you."

The Beer Men

After a Beer Festival in London, all the brewery presidents decided to go out for a beer.

Corona's president sits down and says, "Señor, I would like the world's best beer, a Corona."

The bartender takes a bottle from the shelf and gives it to him.

Then Budweiser's president says, "I'd like the best beer in the world, give me 'The King of Beers', a Budweiser."

The bartender gives him one.

Coors' president says, "I'd like the best beer in the world, the only one made with Rocky Mountain spring water. Give me a Coors."

He gets it.

The guy from Guinness sits down and says, "Give me a Coke."

The other brewery presidents look over at him, shocked, and ask, "Why aren't you drinking a Guinness?

The Guinness president replies, "Well, if you guys aren't drinking beer, neither will I."

Discrimination in Action

A blonde walked into an electronics store and said to the salesman, "I want that TV."

The salesman shook his head and said, "No, we don't sell to blondes."

So the blonde left and came back with her hair dyed brown and said, "I'll take that TV."

Again the salesman said, "Nope, we don't sell to

So she left again and came back with her hair dyed black and said, "I want that TV."

But the salesman just chuckled and said, "No, we don't sell to blondes."

Finally the blonde got fed up and said, "That's it! How'd you know I'm a blonde?!"

The salesman answered, "Because that's a microwave."

Helpful Wife

A male driver sees flashing lights behind him and pulls over and rolls down his window.

"What's the problem, officer?" he asked.

The office leaned over and said, "Sir, you were going 75 in a 55 zone."

"No sir, I was going 55," the man insisted.

The man's wife in the passenger seat rolls her eyes and says, "Come on, Jake. You were going 80."

The man gives his wife a dirty look.

"I'm also going to give you a ticket for your broken tail light," the police officer added.

"Broken tail light? I didn't know I had a broken tail light!"

His wife interjected, "Nonsense, Jake, you've known about that tail light for weeks."

The man gives his wife another dirty look.

The police officer the says, "I'm also going to give you a citation for not wearing your seat belt."

"Oh, no, no, no, I just took it off when you were walking up to the car to get my wallet out," the driver insisted.

But his wife says, "Jake, you know you never wear your seat belt."

The driver, exasperated, says, "Damnit, shut up, woman!"

The police officer says to the woman, "Ma'am, does your husband always talk to you this way?"

The woman responds, "No, officer, only when he's drunk."

The Confession

A middle-aged man went to church to confess his sins.

He said to the priest, "Father, yesterday I sinned with a beautiful young woman."

The priest said, "Here's what you need to do: go get twenty lemons. Squeeze all the juice from the lemons, and then drink the juice."

"And then I'll be forgiven for my sins?" the man asked.

"Oh, no," said the priest, "but it'll get that stupid grin off your face."

The Outhouse

There was a cowboy who went to the outhouse.

Alone in the dark outhouse, he heard a noise, so he looked down between his legs. Lo and behold, there was an Indian down in the hole.

The cowboy said, "How long have you been down there in that awful hole, Chief?"

The Indian looked up through the hole and replied sadly, "Many moons."

False Teeth

A old man coughed violently, and his false teeth shot across the room and smashed against the wall.

"Oh, no," he said, looking down at his broken false teeth, "what do I do now? I can't afford a new set."

"Don't worry," said his friend. "I'll get a pair from my brother for you."

The next day the friend came back with the teeth, which fit perfectly.

"This is wonderful," said the man. "Your brother must be a very good dentist."

"Oh, he's not a dentist," replied the friend, "he's an undertaker."

Second Wife

A husband and wife were golfing when the wife asked, "Honey, if I died would you get married again?"

The husband thought about it and said, "Well, I guess so, after some time. I mean, I'm still young, right?"

As they walked down the fairway, the woman asked, "Would you let her live in our house?"

And the man replied, "Well, sure, I mean, it's a nice house and all."

After putting, she asked, "Would you let her drive my car?"

The man shrugged, "Sure, why not? It's practically brand new and in great shape."

Finally the wife asked, "Would you let her use my golf clubs?"

And the husband replied, "No, she's left handed."

The Prescription

A nice, calm, and respectable lady walked into the pharmacy, stepped right up to the pharmacy counter, looked straight into the pharmacist's eyes and said, "I would like to buy some cyanide."

The pharmacist asked, "Why in the world do you need cyanide?"

The lady replied, "I need it to poison my husband."

The pharmacist's eyes got big and he exclaimed, "What? I can't give you cyanide to kill your husband! That's against the law! I'll lose my license! They'll throw both of us in jail! All kinds of bad things will happen. Absolutely not! You CANNOT have any cyanide!"

The lady reached into her purse and pulled out a picture of her husband in bed with the pharmacist's wife.

The pharmacist looked at the picture and replied, "Well now. That's different. You didn't tell me you had a prescription."

The Secret to Marital Bliss

At a weekly marriage seminar for husbands, men attend to learn techniques to keep their marriages strong. At the session last week, the counselor asked an old man who was approaching his 50th wedding anniversary to take a few minutes and share some insights into how he had managed to stay married to the same woman all these years.

The old man said to the assembled husbands, "Well, I've tried to treat her nice, buy her things she needs, but, honestly, best of all, I took her to Italy for our 25th anniversary!"

The counselor responded, "Fifty years! You're an amazing inspiration to all the husbands here! Please tell us what you are planning for your wife for your 50th anniversary?"

He proudly replied, "I'm gonna go pick her up from Italy."

The Beauty

Sarah was a very beautiful, very popular young woman. When she got engaged, she constantly reminded her fiancé of her popularity.

"A lot of men will be totally miserable when I marry," she told him.

"Really?" asked the exasperated fiancé, "And just how many men are you planning to marry?"

Big City Lawyer

A rich lawyer from New York City went duck hunting in rural North Dakota. He shot and dropped a bird, but it fell into a farmer's field on the other side of a fence.

As the lawyer climbed over the fence, an elderly farmer drove up on his tractor and asked him what he was doing.

The lawyer responded, "I shot a duck and it fell in this field, and now I'm going to retrieve it."

The old farmer replied, "Nope, this is my property, and you are not coming over here."

The indignant lawyer said, "I am one of the best trial lawyers in New York and if you don't let me get that duck, I'll sue you and take everything you own."

The old farmer smiled and said, "Apparently, you don't know how we settle disputes in North Dakota. We settle small disagreements like this with the 'Three Kick Rule.'

The lawyer scoffed, "And what is the 'Three Kick Rule'?"

The Farmer replied, "Well, we take turns kicking each other until one of us gives up. Because the dispute occurs on my land, I get to go first. I kick you three times and then you kick me three times and so on back and forth until someone gives up."

The lawyer thought about the proposed contest and decided that he could easily take the old codger. He agreed to abide by the local custom. The old farmer slowly climbed down from the tractor and walked up to the attorney.

The old farmer launched his first kick and planted the toe of his heavy steel-toed work boot into the lawyer's groin and dropped him to his knees!

His second kick to the ribs made the lawyer gasp for breath as his side exploded in pain.

The lawyer was on all fours when the farmer's third kick landed on his rear end, sent him face-first into a fresh cow pie.

Summoning every bit of his will and remaining strength, the lawyer very slowly managed to get to his feet.

Wiping his face with the arm of his jacket, he said with a malevolent smirk, "Okay, you old fart. Now it's my turn."

The old farmer smiled and said, "Nah, I give up. You can have the duck."

The Crusaders

All the bravest knights were leaving for the Crusades, knowing that many of them would never return alive.

One knight told his best friend, "My bride is without doubt one of the most beautiful women in the world. It would be a terrible waste if no man could have her. Therefore, as my best and most trusted friend, I am leaving you the key to her chastity belt to use should I not return from the Crusade."

The company of knights were only a mile or so out of town when they noticed a cloud of dust approaching. Thinking it might be an important message from the town, the column halted.

A horseman approached. It was the knight's best friend.

He yells, "Hey, you gave me the wrong key!!"

The Happy Day

"Congratulations, my boy!" said the groom's uncle. "I'm sure you'll look back and remember today as the happiest day of your life."

"But I'm not getting married until tomorrow," protested his nephew.

"I know," replied the uncle.

The Naughty List

When I was a kid, one year Santa gave me a lump of coal in my stocking.

The next year, I poisoned his cookies.

Somehow that old Elf found out and killed my dad.

The First Grade

A group of young children were just getting accustomed to the first grade. The biggest hurdle they faced was that their teacher insisted on no baby talk.

"You need to use 'big people' words," she'd always remind them.

She asked Chris what he had done over the weekend.

"I went to visit my Nana."

"No, you went to visit your *grandmother*. Use big people words!"

She then asked Mitchell what he had done.

"I took a ride on a choo-choo."

She said, "No, you took a ride on a *train*. Use big people words."

She then asked Jack what he had done.

"I read a book," he replied.

"That's wonderful!" the teacher said. "What book did you read?"

Jack thought about it, considered his words carefully, and then puffed out his little chest with great pride and said, "Winnie the *Sh*t*."

A Cold Night

A man on a business trip in the dead of winter wakes up to a text message from his wife back home reading, "Windows frozen won't open."

The man texts back, "Pour some lukewarm water over it and then gently tap the edge with hammer."

Ten minutes later, his wife texts back, "Computer really messed up now."

Homework

A boy working on his homework struggles to think of a word to use in an essay, so he asks his father, "Papa, what is the person called who brings you in contact with the spirit world?"

"A bartender, my boy."

Marriage Lesson

Getting married is very much like going to a restaurant with friends. You order what you want, and when you see what the other guy has, you wish you'd ordered that.

The Interview

The job interviewer asked the young Millennial candidate, "And where would you see yourself in five years?"

The candidate responded, "Personally, I believe my biggest weakness is in listening."

The Game

A man boarded a plane for a long overnight flight from New York to London. He was looking forward to getting some sleep on the overnight flight so he'd be well-rested when he landed, because it would be morning in London when the plane got in.

Unfortunately, the woman who settled into the seat next to him was the very talkative sort. After some polite small talk, the man adjusted his pillow and closed his eyes. But the woman nudged him awake.

"Want to play a game?" she asked.

"No, I'm going to get some sleep," he said, as politely as he could.

He closed his eyes again. But only moments later, he felt a tap on his arm.

"Are you sure you don't want to play a game?"

The man sighed and said, "What kind of game?"

"It's simple and easy!" she explained. "I ask you a question, and if you don't know the answer, you pay me $5. Then you ask me a question."

Again, he declines and tries to get some sleep.

The woman, now agitated, says, "Okay, if you don't know the answer you pay me $5, but if I don't know the answer, I will pay you $500."

This catches the man's attention and, figuring there will be no end to this torment unless he plays, he agrees to the game.

The woman asks the first question.

"What's the distance from the earth to the moon?"

The man doesn't say a word, reaches into his wallet, pulls out a $5 bill and hands it to the woman.

"Okay," says the woman excitedly, "your turn."

A little grumpy, the man thinks for a moment, and then asks the woman, "As I was going to St. Ives, I met a man with seven wives. Each wife had seven sacks, each sack had seven cats. Each cat had seven kits. Kits, cats, sacks, and wives, how many were there going to St. Ives?"

The woman, puzzled by the riddle, starts to think about it. The man nods off next to her as she investigates.

Noticing he's asleep, she takes out her phone, connects to the plane's wifi, and Googles the riddle. But every answer she finds is ambiguous. Is the answer one, because only the narrator says he's going to St. Ives? Or does the question mean how many people, but not sacks? There are so many potential answers. Frustrated, she texts her friends and then her coworkers, to no avail.

After an hour, she wakes the man and hands him $500 in defeat.

The man says, "Thanks," puts the cash in his wallet, puts his head on the pillow, and goes back to sleep.

The woman, who is now more than a little miffed, wakes the man once again and asks, "Well, what's the answer?"

Without a word, the man opens his wallet, hands the woman $5, and goes back to sleep.

Fifty Short Funnies

1. I got another letter from a creditor today. It said, "Final Notice".

    Good to know they won't bother me anymore.

2. I dreamt I was forced to eat a giant marshmallow. When I woke up, my pillow was gone.

3. An eskimo brings his friend to his home for a visit. When they arrive, there's nothing but a snowy field.

    His friend, puzzled, asks, "So, where's your igloo?"

    The friend replies, "Oh, no! I must've left the iron on!"

4. A worried mother asks her son, "Andy, do you think I'm a bad mom?"

   Her son responded, "My name is Chad."

5. A doctor said to his patient, "You're obese."

   The patient, insulted, responded, "For that I definitely want a second opinion."

   So the doctor said, "You're quite ugly, too."

6. If you write a suicide note that rhymes, it also works as a country-western song.

7. Today at the bank, an old lady asked me to help check her balance. So I pushed her over.

8. A computer once beat me at chess, but it was no match for me at kick boxing.

9. I bought some shoes from a drug dealer. I don't know what he laced them with, but I've been tripping all day.

10. What do you call a boomerang that doesn't come back? A stick.

11. I told my girlfriend she drew her eyebrows too high. She seemed surprised.

12. My dog used to chase people on a bike a lot. It got so bad, I had to take his bike away.

13. I'm so good at sleeping. I can do it with my eyes closed.

14. My boss told me to have a good day, so I went home.

15. One eye said to the other, "Between the two of us, something smells."

16. A woman walked into a library and asked if they had any books about paranoia. The librarian said, "They're right behind you!"

17. The other day, my wife asked me to pass her lipstick, but I accidentally passed her a glue stick. She still isn't talking to me.

18. Why do blind people hate skydiving? It scares the hell out of their dogs.

19. When you look really closely, all mirrors look like eyeballs.

20. My friend says to me: "What rhymes with orange?" I said, "No, it doesn't."

21. What do you call a guy with a rubber toe? Roberto.

22. What did the pirate say when he turned 80 years old? Aye matey.

23. My wife told me I had to stop acting like a flamingo. So I had to put my foot down.

24. I couldn't figure out why the baseball kept getting larger. Then it hit me.

25. Why did the old man fall in the well? Because he couldn't see that well.

26. I ate a clock yesterday, it was very time consuming.

27. Whatdya call a frenchman wearing sandals? Phillipe Phillope.

28. A blind man walks into a bar. And a table. And a chair.

29. I know a lot of jokes about unemployed people but none of them work.

30. What's orange and sounds like a parrot? A carrot.

31. Did you hear about the Italian chef that died? He pasta way.

32. Why couldn't the bicycle stand up? Because it was two tired!

33. Parallel lines have so much in common. It's a shame they'll never meet.

34. My wife accused me of being immature. I told her to get out of my fort.

35. Where do you find a cow with no legs? Right where you left it.

36. When a deaf person sees someone yawn, do they think it's a scream?

37. As I suspected, someone has been adding soil to my garden. The plot thickens.

38. And the Lord said unto John, "Come forth and you will receive eternal life". John came fifth and received a toaster.

39. How does Darth Vader like his toast? On the dark side.

40. When will the little snake arrive? I don't know, but he won't be long...

41. What has three letters and starts with gas? A car.

42. I think i would like a job cleaning mirrors, it's just something I could really see myself doing.

43. Why did it take so long for the pirates to learn the Alphabet? They got stuck at C.

44. I took the shell off my racing snail thinking it would make him go faster, if anything it made him more sluggish.

45. Somebody stole my Microsoft Office and they're going to pay. You have my Word.

46. Just remember: you are never really completely useless; you can always serve as a bad example.

47. I just wrote a book on reverse psychology. Do *not* read it!

48. What did one hat say to the other? You stay here. I'll go on ahead.

49. Why wouldn't the shrimp share his treasure? Because he was a little shellfish.

50. Two cows are standing in a field.

One cow says to the other, "Did you hear about that outbreak of mad cow disease? It makes cows go completely insane!"

The other cow replies, "Good thing I'm a helicopter."

Made in the USA
Middletown, DE
07 November 2024